For Alyssa

Contents

Chapter One

The Flying Horse

"There!" said the nurse with the blue belt, looking proudly at the hard white plaster on Ellen's right arm. "All ready for your friends to write their names on it."

Ellen had fallen off her bike and broken her arm, and Mum had taken her to hospital. The arm wasn't hurting nearly as much as it had at first, and Ellen liked the idea of her friends writing their names on the plaster.

"Can I go back to school tomorrow?" she asked eagerly.

"No," said the nurse. "The doctor wants you to stay in hospital tonight, just so we can keep an eye on you. It's because you had concussion."

"What's that?"

"It's when you bang your head and forget things."

It was true that Ellen's head had hit the pavement when she fell off her bike, and for a minute or so she hadn't been able to

remember where she was or what had happened.

"I'm always telling her to wear her cycle helmet," said Mum to the nurse.

Ellen looked at the floor and felt guilty. "Sorry," she muttered. "But I feel fine now."

"All the same, we need to keep you in to be on the safe side." The nurse turned to Mum and added, "I expect you'll be able to take her home tomorrow, after the doctor's done his ward round."

A porter appeared with a wheelchair. "Sit in this, old lady," he said to Ellen, and, "You'll have to walk, young lady," to Mum.

It seemed strange to Ellen that she should need a wheelchair when it was her arm and not her leg that she had broken, but she was too shy to say so. The porter wheeled her in and out of a lift and then along a corridor into a room with six beds in it.

"This is Jupiter Ward," he said. "You'll get five-star treatment in here." He parked the wheelchair at the reception desk.

A nurse with a red belt welcomed Ellen and Mum. "I'm Sister Jo," she told them. She showed Ellen her bed, which had a curtain you could draw all round it. Then she fitted a plastic bracelet on to Ellen's left wrist. It had her name on it.

"You'll need to put these on too." Sister Jo was holding out some hospital pyjamas.

"But how will I get the top on over the plaster?" Ellen asked.

"Don't worry – we think of everything,"

said Sister Jo. When Mum helped Ellen put the pyjamas on they found that the right sleeve had been cut off and the armhole widened so that the plaster could fit through it.

"I'd better go back home now," said Mum.

Ellen felt a bit scared. "I don't want you to go," she said.

"You'll be fine. It's only for one night. And I'm sure you'll make friends with the other children."

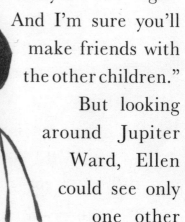

But looking around Jupiter Ward, Ellen could see only one other child, a boy who was asleep. Three of the beds were empty and the other one had its curtains drawn around it.

"Hardly anyone seems to be breaking any bones these days," said Sister Jo. "If it wasn't for you, Ellen, I might lose my job!"

Ellen smiled, and found she felt less scared. She hugged Mum goodbye with her left arm and made her promise to bring in a bunch of grapes and a library book the next day.

"Now, down to business," said Sister Jo when Mum had gone. "You need to choose what you want to eat tomorrow. Are you left-handed by any chance?"

"No," said Ellen, puzzled. "Do you do different meals for left-handed people then?"

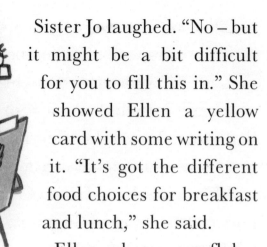

Sister Jo laughed. "No – but it might be a bit difficult for you to fill this in." She showed Ellen a yellow card with some writing on it. "It's got the different food choices for breakfast and lunch," she said.

Ellen chose cornflakes and orange juice for breakfast, and chicken pie and fruit salad for lunch. Sister Jo ticked the boxes for her.

"I'm going off duty now," she said. "I'll be back tomorrow lunchtime, but you might be gone by then."

Ellen was sorry to see Sister Jo go. Another nurse took her temperature, and then a different one brought her some cocoa and yet another one took her to the bathroom. It was bewildering having so many different people to look after her and Ellen suddenly felt tired. One of the nurses tucked her up in her new bed.

"Just ring this bell if you want anything in the night," she said.

Ellen was woken by a light tap on her shoulder. At first she thought it was Mum, but then she opened her eyes, saw the nurse and remembered where she was. Although she hadn't felt ill enough to ring the bell, it hadn't been a good night. Because of the plaster she couldn't sleep on her right side like she usually did, and it was hard to find a comfortable position. Then she had been woken up very early to have her temperature taken, after which she had fallen into a much deeper sleep.

"We couldn't wake you up when the breakfast trolley came round," the nurse said now. "But don't worry – we've saved yours for you. You should have time to eat it before Doctor Birch comes."

"Have I got time to go to the bathroom too?" asked Ellen.

"Yes. Do you want someone to come and help you?"

"No, thanks." But once Ellen was in the bathroom she found it was quite awkward washing and cleaning her teeth with only her left hand.

"I'll have to learn to write left-handed too," she said aloud.

"That's a good idea," came a voice from the bathroom mirror. "Who knows? That way you might start doing the letters the right way round at last."

Ellen knew that voice very well. It belonged to Princess Mirror-Belle.

Princess Mirror-Belle looked just like Ellen's reflection, but whereas most

reflections stay in the mirror, Mirror-
Belle had a habit of coming out of it.
Although she looked like Ellen, she was
not at all like her in character. Ellen was
quite shy, but Mirror-Belle was extremely

boastful and was full of stories about the palace and the fairy-tale land she said she came from.

Mirror-Belle was dressed in hospital pyjamas just like Ellen, but her plaster was on her left arm.

"Well, don't just stand there staring," she said. "I'll need a bit of help getting out of here." She stuck her right arm out of the mirror and added, "Don't pull too hard. I don't want to break this one as well."

Although Ellen wasn't really sure that she wanted Mirror-Belle in hospital with her, it seemed too late to change things, so she grasped her hand and helped her to wriggle out on to the washbasin and down to the floor. "Did you fall off your bike too?" she asked.

"Certainly not," replied Mirror-Belle. "Would you expect a princess to ride around on anything as common as a bicycle? No . . ." She hesitated for a second and then went on, "I fell off my flying horse."

"You never told me you had a flying horse."

"Well, I'm sorry, Ellen, but I can't tell you all the things I have. It would take too long and it would just make you jealous."

"Were you wearing a riding hat?" asked Ellen. But Mirror-Belle wasn't listening. She had opened the bathroom door and was sauntering into Jupiter Ward.

Ellen was about to follow her, but then decided to hang back. Somehow

she couldn't face trying to explain to the nurses about Mirror-Belle.

She peeped out of the bathroom door and saw her mirror friend climbing into her own bed and ringing the bell above it.

One of the nurses came scurrying to her bedside.

"What is this food supposed to be?" Mirror-Belle asked, pointing to the

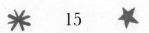

breakfast tray on the table beside her bed.

"It's what you ordered. Cornflakes and orange juice."

"Cornflakes? What are they? Take them away and bring me a  lightly boiled peacock's egg."

The nurse tittered. She seemed to think this was a joke.

"Don't laugh when I'm giving you your orders," said Mirror-Belle. "It's very rude. You can take the orange juice away too. I'd rather have a glass of fresh morning dew with ice and lemon."

"You're not getting anything else," said the nurse. "Anway, the breakfast trolley's gone now."

"Then call it back again this second."

The nurse picked up the untouched breakfast tray and scurried off with it, nearly bumping into a man in a white coat with a stethoscope round his neck. Ellen guessed that he must be Dr Birch.

"I think she's taken a turn for the worse," murmured the nurse with the tray.

The doctor went over to the bed and drew the curtains round it. Ellen, still peeping out of the bathroom, couldn't see him any longer, but she heard his voice.

"It's Ellen, isn't it?" the doctor was saying.

"No, it's Princess Mirror-Belle. I hope you're properly trained to look after royalty. That stethoscope looks very ordinary. The palace doctor has one made of silver and snakeskin."

Dr Birch chuckled. "My little niece likes playing princesses too," he said. "Very well, Your Royal Highness. Now, I want you to tell me everything you can remember about your accident. I see from your notes that you fell off your bike."

"Then your notes are wrong," said Mirror-Belle. "I fell off my flying horse. I'm a very good rider, actually, so I can't quite think how it happened. I suspect that my wicked fairy godmother was up to her tricks again – loosening the saddle or something."

"So you have no memory of any bike ride? Maybe that's because you banged your head on the pavement."

"I did no such thing!" said Mirror-Belle indignantly. "There aren't any pavements where I live. I landed . . . um . . . in a stork's nest on the palace roof. Luckily there weren't any stork's eggs in it at the time, otherwise—"

"Just a minute!" interrupted the doctor. His voice sounded quite different suddenly – urgent and excited. "It says

here that you broke your right arm."

"I do wish you'd stop reading those stupid notes and listen to me instead," complained Mirror-Belle.

"It's not just the notes. The  X-ray shows it quite clearly too. The right arm was broken, but they've plastered the left one!"

"It sounds as if you should sack the plasterer as well as the note-taker."

"How does your right arm feel? Does it still hurt?"

"Now you mention it, it is a little sore. I think that must be from where the storks pecked it. They didn't realize who I was, you see. They probably thought I was a cuckoo who was about to lay its egg in their nest."

Doctor Birch obviously wasn't interested in storks or cuckoos, because Ellen saw him emerge from behind the curtains, almost run to the reception desk and pick up the telephone. His back was turned and Ellen could only catch a few words, such as "mistake", "urgent" and "emergency". She guessed that he was speaking to someone in the plaster room.

This had gone too far, Ellen decided. She really ought to explain everything to the doctor and nurses. She was just braving herself to stride out from the bathroom when she saw someone familiar come into Jupiter Ward. It was the same porter who had wheeled her there yesterday, and he was pushing an empty wheelchair.

"You again, old lady?" she heard him say to Mirror-Belle.

Ellen didn't think Mirror-Belle would like being called "old lady" and expected her to tell the nice porter off, but instead Mirror-Belle answered, "Ah – at least someone recognizes that I'm not just an ordinary little girl. And I'm delighted to see that you've brought this splendid throne for me. Even the palace thrones don't have wheels!"

"Nothing but the best for you, old lady,"

said the porter, and he wheeled her out of Jupiter Ward.

Oh dear! Ellen had to stop this. If Mirror-Belle's left arm really was broken, it wouldn't do for the plaster to be taken off.

Maybe the easiest person to explain things to would be the nice porter. Ellen stepped out of the bathroom and glanced around the ward. The doctor was talking to the nurse at the reception desk. They were gazing deeply into each other's eyes and didn't notice Ellen as she slipped out of the ward. She was just in time to see the porter pushing Mirror-Belle into a lift.

"Stop!" she cried, but the doors had already slid closed.

There was another lift and Ellen pressed the button to call it. It took a long time to come, but at least it was empty when it arrived, so no one could give her funny looks or ask what she was doing on her own.

If the plaster room was where her own arm had been plastered, Ellen was pretty sure it was on the ground floor, so she pressed the G button. But when the lift stopped and she got out, there was no sign of Mirror-Belle or the porter. Ellen found herself in a long corridor with lots of doors leading off it. She looked at the notices on some of the doors but they weren't much help because she couldn't understand what the words meant: one said "Endocrinology", another said "Haematology" and a third "Toxicology". Ellen was just wondering whether one of these "ology" words was a special medical way of writing "plaster room" when the Haematology door swung open and a nurse with a purple belt came out.

"Can I help you?" she asked Ellen. She looked and sounded quite kind.

"I'm looking for the plaster room," said Ellen.

"Isn't anyone with you? Where have you come from?"

Ellen hesitated, wondering what to tell the nurse. She decided on the truth, even though she doubted if she would be believed.

"I've come from Jupiter Ward," she said, "but they don't know I'm here. You see, they thought my friend Princess Mirror-Belle was me. The thing is, Mirror-Belle broke her left arm but—"

"Just a minute," Purple Belt interrupted her. "Perhaps I'd better phone Jupiter Ward and see what's going on." She took Ellen to an office with a phone in it.

"I think I've got a patient of yours

here." Purple Belt took Ellen's left hand and read the identity bracelet round her wrist. "She's called Ellen Page, and she says she's supposed to be in the plaster room . . . That's all right then; I just wanted to check, because she seems a bit confused . . . talking about princesses and things like that . . . oh, I see – concussion; yes, that would fit . . . No, it's OK, I can take her there myself."

Purple Belt put down the phone and smiled brightly at Ellen. "They offered to send another porter, but it's only just round the corner," she said. She took Ellen to a door with a couple of chairs outside it.

Ellen knew she was in the right place

because she could hear a familiar voice from inside the room: "My horse's name is Little Lord Lightning. Unfortunately he's been suffering from wing-ache recently. I really ought to take him to the palace vet."

Purple Belt smiled at Ellen and rolled her eyes. "You might have a bit of a wait. It sounds as if there's quite a difficult patient in there."

Ellen decided against saying, "It's Princess Mirror-Belle." Purple Belt would just think she was still confused. Instead she answered, "I don't mind waiting."

"Goodbye then," said Purple Belt. "You won't wander off, will you?"

"No," promised Ellen, sitting down on one of the chairs. She watched Purple Belt disappear down the corridor. Now that she had tracked Mirror-Belle down she found she was dreading the idea of barging into the plaster room and explaining everything to the nurse in there.

"That's funny," came a voice from the room, interrupting Mirror-Belle's account of her flying horse. "I can't read the name on your bracelet. The letters look kind of back to front. I'd better go and get my reading glasses – they're in my coat pocket." A nurse came out of the room. It wasn't the same one who had put Ellen's arm in plaster, though she had a blue belt like hers.

The nurse hurried down the corridor and Ellen, relieved at this chance to talk to Mirror-Belle on her own, slipped into the room.

Mirror-Belle was standing by the window, holding a large pair of scissors in her right hand. "Oh, hello, Ellen," she said. "Do you think these scissors are really suitable for cutting a royal plaster? They look rather poor quality to me. I thought I might try them out on a few things myself before the servant returns." She aimed the scissors at the curtains.

"Stop!" cried Ellen. She grabbed the scissors from Mirror-Belle. "The nurse will be back in a second and you've got to go!" she told her.

"Don't you start ordering me around, Ellen," Mirror-Belle reproached her. "You're getting to be as bad as your servants. I'll come and go as I please."

"But surely you don't want to stay and have your plaster cut off? If you've broken your arm, you need it."

"Good point," said Mirror-Belle. "Now you're talking sense. Perhaps I should go back and see how Little Lord Lightning is getting on. Besides, no one here seems to have any respect for royalty – except for the throne-pusher, that is. He was extremely polite. I might see if I can find a job for him in the palace."

"Mirror-Belle, just go – please!" Ellen begged.

"All in good time," replied Mirror-Belle. She picked up a pen from a table.

"What are you doing now?" Ellen felt rattled. Everything would be so much easier if Mirror-Belle had gone by the time Blue Belt came back.

In reply, Mirror-Belle held the pen out to her. "As a special honour, I'm going to allow you to be the first person to sign my plaster," she said.

There was obviously no wriggling out of this, so Ellen took the pen and wrote her name as well as she could with her left hand.

"Really, Ellen, this is even worse than your normal writing. As well as being backwards, the letters are awfully wobbly."

"They're not backwards – and they only look wobbly because I'm writing left-handed."

"I'll show you how it should be done," said Mirror-Belle, taking the pen from

Ellen. She wrote her own name on Ellen's plaster. It looked like this:

Mirror_Belle

"Talk about backwards and wobbly," Ellen couldn't help muttering, even though there wasn't time for an argument. She glanced round the room, hoping to see a mirror, but there was none.

Just then they heard footsteps in the corridor. Blue Belt was coming back!

"Farewell!" cried Mirror-Belle, and she darted out of the door. Ellen peered out and saw her go through a door on the other side of the corridor. It had another of the long "ology" words written on it. "Ophthalmology," this one said.

"Now, now," said Blue Belt, coming into

the plaster room. "You were supposed to stay sitting down. It's funny," she added, "I thought for a moment that I saw you going into the eye department, but it must have been someone else."

She put on her reading glasses and looked at Ellen's identity bracelet.

"That's good – I can read it fine now," she said. "Ellen Page." She checked the name against Ellen's notes, and then frowned. "There's no problem with the name, but I can't understand what the doctor's written. It says, 'Remove plaster from left arm and plaster right arm,' but your right arm is plastered. I suppose he must mean, 'Remove plaster from right arm and plaster left arm'."

"No, no!" exclaimed Ellen in alarm. "It's the right one that's broken. The left one works fine." She waved it about to prove her point. Blue Belt checked the notes and the X-ray.

"Well, it's all very strange," she said. "I do wonder if that Doctor Birch's mind is always on his work."

She phoned for a porter to take Ellen back to Jupiter Ward and then frowned again. "It's funny," she said, "but I could have sworn the plaster was on your left arm too! Before I fetched my glasses, that is. I really ought to pop into the eye department and get my sight checked."

At that moment there was a babble of voices in the corridor and someone knocked on the door. Blue Belt opened it, and Ellen heard three voices speaking at once. As far as she could make out, a woman was asking, "Is she in here?" and a boy was saying, "I keep telling you what happened," and a man was saying, "Be quiet, Toby."

"I'm sorry – who are you looking for?" asked Blue Belt.

"I don't even know her name, but I thought she might have been one of your patients," came the woman's voice. "I was just checking little Toby's eyesight – you know, that test where they have to read the letters in the mirror – and this girl with her arm in plaster came charging in. She was talking a lot of nonsense, something about all the letters being back to front. She refused to leave when I asked her to, so I went to get the doctor to help me, but when we got back she'd just disappeared."

"Yes – into the mirror!" came the boy's voice.

"Don't be silly, Toby. You know that's impossible," said the man.

"But I saw her!"

"Yes, but don't forget you need new glasses."

"Well, I'm sorry," said Blue Belt, "but whoever she is, she's not in here."

Ellen had found a blanket and covered herself with it, terrified that the people outside would come in, see her and accuse her of Mirror-Belle's bad behaviour. But they seemed happy to accept what Blue Belt said, and she heard the woman saying,

"Maybe she belongs on Jupiter Ward. I'll try phoning them."

Blue Belt shook her head when they had gone. "Everybody seems to be going mad today," she said. "Except you, Charlie," she added to the nice porter who had just come into the room.

"Hello, old lady – has that naughty nurse been drawing pictures on your plaster?" he said to Ellen. Ellen smiled faintly and sat down in the wheelchair.

"You've gone all quiet," he told her as he pushed her into the lift. "Aren't you going to tell me any more stories about your flying horse?" Ellen just shook her head and closed her eyes. She suddenly felt very tired.

Back in Jupiter Ward, two friendly

people were there to greet her – Sister Jo and Mum. Mum was looking quite worried. "I hear you've been a bit delirious," she said.

"No, I'm fine," said Ellen.

"If you ask me," said Sister Jo in a low voice, "it's that Doctor Birch who's been a bit delirious. Fancy not knowing his right from his left! I think he must be in love. I'm going to ask Doctor Hamza to see you as soon as you've had your lunch. You must be starving – I gather you didn't fancy your breakfast."

"That's not like you, Ellen," said Mum.

Ellen, who didn't feel like explaining, gobbled up her chicken pie and fruit salad. She was halfway through the bunch of grapes that Mum had brought in when Dr Hamza appeared at her bedside. He asked her about her fall and got her to count backwards from a hundred to fifty.

"She seems very fine and dandy to me," he told Mum. "You can take her home."

Mum had brought in some new clothes, including a blouse with a cut-off sleeve like the hospital pyjama top. She helped Ellen into them.

"Do you want to pop into the bath-room before you go?" asked Sister Jo. "Then you can see in the mirror how smart you look."

"No!" said Ellen. "I mean, no, thank you. Can I go back to school now and show everyone the plaster?"

"That can wait till tomorrow," said Mum. "I think you should take things easy this afternoon. You can finish the grapes and read the new library book I've got out for you."

"What's it called?" asked Ellen.

"*The Flying Horse*," said Mum, and couldn't understand why Ellen laughed all the way down in the lift.

Chapter Two

The Magic Ball

"Don't get too many yellow cards, Ellen!" said Dad.

Ellen's big brother Luke chortled at this, but Ellen just smiled thinly. "I might not even play football," she said. "There are lots of other sports you can choose."

The leisure centre was having an open day. Dad and Luke were going to play a game of squash, and Ellen was doing something called "Four for Free", which

meant you could try out four sports without paying anything.

"We'll be on squash court three," said Dad. "Just in case you need me to sort out any refs for you!" he added.

Luke chuckled again. "I think I'd better do that, Dad. You won't be in a fit state after I've beaten you!" Then the two of them strode off, swinging their rackets jauntily.

Ellen decided to try out the Eight and Over gym first. It didn't have any weight-lifting machines like the big gym, but it did have a trampoline and some running and cycling machines.

She showed her Four for Free card

to the muscular young attendant in the gym. He ticked one of the boxes on it and handed it back to her.

The gym was very busy but Ellen found a free running machine. She'd never been on one before so the attendant had to show her how to use it.

It felt strange at first to run on the spot. Ellen was just getting the hang of it when she heard a voice saying, "You're going the wrong way!"

Ellen had been concentrating so hard on her feet and the

little screen showing her speed that she had hardly taken in the row of mirrors facing the running machines. Startled by the voice, she stopped running.

Her reflection stopped just as suddenly – except, of course, that it wasn't really her reflection; it was Princess Mirror-Belle.

"Mirror-Belle! What are you doing here?" asked Ellen.

Princess Mirror-Belle jumped off her machine and jogged out of the mirror and into the gym. "Chasing the magic ball," she said. "Have you seen it?"

Ellen looked round. She couldn't see a ball, and she was relieved that no one else in the gym seemed to have noticed Mirror-Belle; they were all too busy

bouncing and running or cycling.

"What magic ball?" she asked.

"The one my wicked fairy godmother threw," said Mirror-Belle. "She's been up to her tricks again. She's turned everyone in the palace to stone."

"Except for you," remarked Ellen.

"Yes, well, she was going to do it to me too, but luckily I knew the special magic words to stop her."

"What were they?"

Mirror-Belle looked rather annoyed, and said, "Don't hold me up – I told you, I have to find the magic ball."

"You still haven't explained about that," said Ellen.

"Haven't I? Well, the wicked fairy threw it and said that the stone spell would only be broken if I could bring it back to her. You should have heard her cackle!"

"Why was she cackling?"

"Because everyone knows that it's almost impossible to keep up with her magic ball. I've  been chasing it for days – through forests and up and down mountains – but it's always just ahead of me. And now I seem to have lost sight of it altogether."

Mirror-Belle glanced round the gym and then her eyes lit up. "Aha!" she said, and she marched up to the muscular attendant.

"You can't fool me," she told him, and she jumped up and tapped his arm.

"Stop mucking about," he said.

"That's no way to talk to a princess," said Mirror-Belle. "And, in any case, you're the one who's mucking about. Roll up your sleeve immediately!"

"Stop it, Mirror-Belle," said Ellen. "You'll get us chucked out."

"But it's perfectly clear he's hiding the magic ball up his sleeve," said Mirror-Belle.

"Don't be silly – that's not a ball, it's just

his arm muscles," said Ellen, laughing.

The attendant looked quite amused and actually did roll up his right sleeve. He was probably glad to have a chance to display his bulging biceps.

Mirror-Belle looked unimpressed and demanded to see the other arm. But by now the attendant had had enough. Perhaps he thought they were trying to make fun of him.

"Why don't you two buzz off and try out something else," he said. Then a suspicious look crossed his face. "Have I ticked both your cards?" he asked.

Ellen showed him hers, and Mirror-Belle also took a card from the pocket of her tracksuit trousers. The attendant stared at it. "That's funny," he said. "The writing's all wrong on this one."

Ellen glanced at Mirror-Belle's card. She was not surprised to see that it was in mirror-writing. Instead of saying FOUR FOR FREE it said:

ƎƎЯꟻ ЯOꟻ ЯUOꟻ

"It's perfectly correct," said Mirror-Belle. "You probably just left school too young, before you'd fully mastered the art of reading." She shook her head and turned to Ellen. "All muscles and no brain," she murmured. Ellen couldn't help giggling.

The attendant was really cross now. "Get out!" he said.

Ellen tugged at Mirror-Belle's arm. "Why don't we have a go at five-a-side football?" she said.

"Football, did you say? That sounds promising!"

To Ellen's relief, Mirror-Belle seemed to forget about the muscular attendant's left arm and she followed Ellen out of the gym and down the stairs.

In the five-a-side hall a woman in a pink tracksuit looked pleased to see them.

"Good – we needed an extra two to get started," she said. "I hope you don't mind being on different teams." After hurriedly checking their cards, she gave Ellen a blue armband and Mirror-Belle a red one and told them where to stand. Then she put a football down in the middle of the pitch.

Mirror-Belle looked disappointed. "That's not the magic ball," she said. "It's too big, and it's the wrong colour. I'll have to search elsewhere."

"Oh, do stay," said Ellen. "Otherwise your team will be one short."

Mirror-Belle shrugged her shoulders. Pink Tracksuit blew a whistle, and everyone started running around, kicking the ball and trying to score goals.

One of the other children on the red team passed the ball to Mirror-Belle and she picked it up. "Thank you," she said, "but it's no use to me. Here, Ellen, catch!" And ignoring Pink Tracksuit, who was blowing her whistle, she threw the ball to Ellen.

The others on the red team started shouting at Mirror-Belle.

"Stupid!"

"You're not allowed to use your hands."

"She's on the othcr side anyway."

Mirror-Belle looked shocked. She went up to Pink Tracksuit. "Excuse me – you seem to be in charge. What is the punishment for being rude to royalty? In my father's kingdom these people would have to weed the palace gardens for a year."

Pink Tracksuit ignored this. "Free kick for the blues," she announced and, "Get back in your place," she told Mirror-Belle.

"Just who do you think you are?" Mirror-Belle asked her.

"I'm the coach," said Pink Tracksuit.

Mirror-Belle started to laugh. "In that case, where are your six white horses? Where are your wheels and your velvet cushions? Where are the driver and the footmen?"

Pink Tracksuit looked as if she might send Mirror-Belle off, and Ellen tried to come to the rescue. "I'm sorry," she said. "I don't think she's ever played football before." She managed to coax Mirror-Belle back on to the pitch. "You have to kick the ball, and only to people in your team – or into the goal," she told her. "That's the net thing," she added, pointing, as Mirror-Belle was looking blank.

Pink Tracksuit blew the whistle and the game started up again. The blue team scored a goal, and then another one. Then the reds got the ball. One of them passed it to Mirror-Belle.

"No – not to her," moaned another red player, but it was too late. Mirror-Belle had given the ball a huge kick. It landed in the red team's goal.

"Yes!" shouted some of the blues,

jumping up and down, but the reds were furious.

"You idiot!"

"That was an own goal!"

"Get her off!"

Once again Mirror-Belle strode up to Pink Tracksuit. "I'm simply not putting up with this petty jealousy," she complained.

"We're not jealous!" said one of the reds.

"Yes, you are. I've just done what those two other people did – kicked the ball into the net – but, if I may say so, with far greater skill and style than they did. I can't help it if the rest of you can't match up to me."

"But it was the wrong goal! You should have kicked it into the blue goal!"

"Really," said Mirror-Belle, "I can't be bothered with all these silly details. You'll just have to play four-a-side. Come on, Ellen, let's go."

Ellen thought this was a good idea, and so did everyone else.

"Well, that was a waste of time," said Mirror-Belle as they left the football hall. "Now maybe I'll never find the magic ball, and my parents and all the servants will remain statues for ever. I suppose in that case I'd have to come and live with you, Ellen."

Ellen wasn't too sure about

this plan. A little of Mirror-Belle went a long way. Luckily she was saved from replying because Mirror-Belle stopped suddenly outside a door and said, "Just a minute, do I hear bouncing? What's in there?"

"It's the indoor tennis courts." Tennis was one of the sports you could choose as part of Four for Free, although after the football experience Ellen wasn't keen for Mirror-Belle to join in.

But she had no choice. Mirror-Belle had already opened the door, and a jolly-looking woman in white shorts and a T-shirt was greeting them.

"Hi there, four-for-frees! Jolly good – now we can play doubles; what fun!" She gave them both tennis rackets and introduced them to two other girls called Jade and Ailsa. Then she asked Ellen, "Do you two want to play together or opposite each other?"

"Together," said Ellen hastily, remembering the disastrous football game.

A lot of yellow tennis balls were lying on the ground and Mirror-Belle was inspecting them. "These are the right colour, but they're too furry, and they're not trying to escape," she said.

The jolly woman laughed heartily. "Now, how about a little knockabout before you start a proper game?" she suggested. "You serve first, Mirror-Belle."

"Naturally," said Mirror-Belle. She picked up a ball and hit it to Ellen.

Jade and Ailsa giggled, and the jolly woman said, "Whoopsadaisy!"

"You're not supposed to pass it to me," said Ellen.

"Why ever not? You're on my team, aren't you?"

"Yes."

"Well, in that other stupid game you said I was to pass the ball to people on the same team. Which is it to be? Do make up your mind – I haven't got all day."

"Well, you see . . ." Ellen was about to explain the difference between football and tennis when Mirror-Belle's face lit up. "Oh, I understand!" she said, and picked up the ball. This time it hit the net. "Goal!" she cried.

Jade and Ailsa giggled some more, but the jolly woman said, "Don't laugh at her. She's doing her best." Then she turned to Mirror-Belle. "Try hitting it a little higher and you'll get it over all right."

"But surely it wouldn't be a goal if it went over the net?" said Mirror-Belle.

"You don't score goals in tennis," Ellen told her. "You have to keep hitting the ball over the net till the other side can't manage to hit it back."

"Well really, this is too tiresome for words. Things are so much simpler back home. When I play with my own golden ball I just throw it and catch it – there's none of this nonsense about teams and goals and nets and red and blue. Occasionally, of course, the ball falls into a pond, but then it usually gets rescued by a frog and I turn him into a prince by kissing him."

The jolly woman laughed again, more uncertainly this time. "I tell you what," she said. "I think you two would enjoy putting. That's quite a straightforward game."

"That's a good idea," said Ellen, but only as a way of getting out of the embarrassing tennis game. She didn't really want to try another sport with Mirror-Belle, and once they were outside in the corridor she said, "Maybe the magic ball has bounced back to your land, Mirror-Belle. Don't you think you ought to go back and look for it there?"

"No, I'm sure it's here somewhere." They had reached the reception area and Mirror-Belle looked around. "What about this butting game? Is there a ball in that?"

"It's putting, not butting," said Ellen, alarmed by the thought of Mirror-Belle trying to head-butt a golf  ball. "Yes, there is a ball, but . . ."

A receptionist overheard them. "Do you want the putting green? Go out through the main door and turn left," she said, and the next second Mirror-Belle was prancing eagerly outside. Ellen followed her doubtfully.

The attendant on the putting green gave them each a club and a ball. Ellen was relieved to find that they could play by themselves, without having to join another group of children.

Mirror-Belle looked disappointed with her ball. "There's nothing magic about this," she said, but she was intrigued by the metal flags sticking out of the ground, each one with a number on it. "How curious," she said. "At home we fly the flag of the kingdom high above the palace. It has a lion and a unicorn on it – except that by now I suppose the wicked fairy must have taken it down and replaced it with her own horrible flag."

"What's that got on it?" asked Ellen.

"Er . . . a spider and a centipede," replied Mirror-Belle. "Still, even that's a bit better than these silly flags in the ground."

"But these ones are different. They're just for the game – to show you where the holes are," Ellen tried to explain.

Instead of listening to her, Mirror-Belle was swinging her golf club about experimentally, as if it was a tennis racket.

"No, not like that. You have to put the ball on the ground, then hit it."

"Get a move on, can't you," came a voice from behind them, and Ellen saw that three boys were queuing up to have a game.

Feeling flustered, she said to Mirror-Belle, "Why don't I go first, so I can show you? I'm not very good, mind."

She stood with her feet apart, swung her club back and gave the ball a smart tap. To her surprise it ended up really near the hole. With a bit of luck she should get it in with the next shot. Ellen felt quite pleased with herself and hoped that the impatient boys were impressed.

But what was Mirror-Belle up to? Instead of placing her own ball on the ground she was running after Ellen's one. And now she was whacking it back in Ellen's direction –

except that it went sailing past her and hit one of the impatient boys.

"What do you think you're doing?" he yelled, clutching his knee.

"Returning the ball, of course," said Mirror-Belle. "And it was a pretty good shot, if you ask me. Ellen here didn't manage to get it back – that's one point to me."

"No, it's not!" Ellen found herself shouting at Mirror-Belle. "I wish you'd listen to me. This isn't tennis, it's putting. It's like golf – you have to get the ball down the hole."

"Well, really!" Mirror-Belle sounded loud and indignant too. "I must say, I thought better of you, Ellen. You keep making me play these stupid games when you know I should be looking for the magic ball, and then you change all the rules to suit yourself."

"No, I don't. And I don't want you to play with me anyway. It was your idea."

"I thought you were my friend," said Mirror-Belle. For the first time ever, Ellen thought she could see tears in her eyes. But she couldn't be sure because the next second Mirror-Belle had thrown down her club and was running away, back towards the main doors of the leisure centre.

"What a nutcase," said the boy with the hurt knee. One of the others seemed to feel sorry for Ellen. "You can play with us if you like," he offered.

"No, it's all right. I'd better make it up with her."

Ellen returned the clubs and balls to the

attendant and then followed in Mirror-Belle's footsteps.

"Have you seen my friend?" she asked the receptionist.

"Oh, I thought she was your twin. Yes, she was here a minute ago. She looked a bit upset. She went into the crèche."

Ellen's heart sank. The crèche was only supposed to be for toddlers and very young children; they could stay there and be looked after while their parents played sports or went to the gym. What on earth was Mirror-Belle up to in there?

She found out as soon as she opened the door and a lightweight blue ball hit her, followed by a red one.

Mirror-Belle was in the ball pool, hurling the balls out of it at a frantic speed. A few excited toddlers were copying her and some others were running around outside the ball pool, picking up the balls and throwing them around. Everyone seemed to be having a good time except for the two women in charge of the crèche. One of them was telling Mirror-Belle off; the other one, seeing Ellen coming in, looked up from the nappy she was changing and said, "Is that girl in the ball

pool your twin? Can you tell her to stop throwing the balls around?"

"She's not, but I'll try," said Ellen and went up to the ball pool.

"Ah, Ellen, there you are at last!" Mirror-Belle greeted her in a friendly voice.

She seemed to have forgotten about their quarrel. "Do you know, that wicked fairy is even more cunning than I thought. She's obviously sent the magic ball in here and she thinks I won't be able to find it among all the others. But I'm sure I'll recognize it. For a start, a lot of them are the wrong colour." She threw a green ball out. "And so far none of the yellow ones feel right. They don't bounce properly." She hurled a couple of yellow balls in different directions. One of them landed softly on the tummy of the baby whose nappy was being changed. He clutched it and burbled happily.

"I expect the magic ball has sunk to the bottom," went on Mirror-Belle. "I'll probably have to get rid of all the others before I find it."

"Mirror-Belle, you've got to stop that! You're not supposed to be in here anyway."

"Who said so? I don't notice any kings or queens around here and they are the only ones who can tell princesses what to do or where to go," said Mirror-Belle.

"But you're too old for the crèche," said Ellen.

"In any case, you have to be signed in by your mother or father," added one of the crèche-workers. She was wearing a badge with a smiley face and the name Tracy on it.

Mirror-Belle looked at her as if she was an idiot. "That's impossible," she said. "As I've already told you, both my parents have been turned to stone."

"Fwo! Fwo! Fwo!" shouted a toddler, eager for some more action. He clamped his arms round one of Mirror-Belle's legs. Obligingly, Mirror-Belle threw a few more balls out of the pool.

Tracy turned to Ellen, hoping to get more sense out of her. "Where are your parents?" she asked.

"Well, my dad's on squash court three," Ellen admitted. "But he's not *her* father," she added hastily.

"Fwo! Fwo!" the toddler started to clamour again, but Mirror-Belle ignored him. "You never told me your father had a court like mine," she said to Ellen in surprise. "How many courtiers does he have waiting on him?"

"It's not that sort of court – not a royal one," said Ellen. "Dad's playing squash with Luke."

"Oh," said Mirror-Belle,

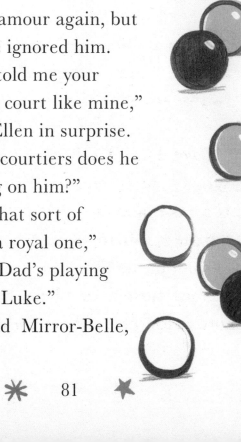

appearing to lose interest. She threw a few more balls around, but rather half-heartedly. Then, all of a sudden, she unclamped the demanding toddler from her leg and sprang out of the ball pool. "I think I've been on the wrong trail all the time," she announced. She ran to the door, flung it open and was gone.

Several little children tottered after her and started crying when Tracy closed the door. The demanding toddler grabbed Ellen's leg and started up his chant of, "Fwo! Fwo! Fwo!" He seemed to expect her to start where Mirror-Belle had left off.

"I'm sorry about all that," said Ellen to Tracy.

"Don't worry," said Tracy. "We can't choose our families."

Ellen decided it would be useless to explain again that Mirror-Belle wasn't related to her. Instead she helped Tracy pick up the scattered balls and throw them back into the ball pool. The toddlers didn't seem to enjoy this nearly as much as they had enjoyed Mirror-Belle throwing them all out, and the crying grew louder.

"Well, I'd better go," said Ellen when the last ball was back in the pool. She wondered where Mirror-Belle had got to but decided not to look for her this time. She would go and find Dad and

Luke on their squash court.

She didn't need to. As soon as she opened the door she saw them outside in the corridor.

"So that's where you've been hiding," said Dad.

Luke was looking cross. "Give it back," he said.

"What are you talking about?" asked Ellen.

"The squash ball, of course. That yellow one was our best one. It was really bouncy."

"But I haven't got it."

"Then what have you done with it?"

"Nothing. I never had it."

"Yes, you did – you came rushing in and snatched it."

"It wasn't me. It must have been Mirror-Belle. She was looking for the magic ball, you see – the one her fairy godmother threw – and—"

"Oh shut up." Luke turned to Dad. "She's always telling whoppers."

But Dad was in a surprisingly good mood. "Ellen's got a vivid imagination, that's all," he said. "And it's not as if that yellow ball was ours anyway. We just found it on the court when we arrived."

Luke didn't want to give up so easily. "She's hidden it in the kids' gym somewhere," he said. "I'm sure I saw her go in there."

Ellen guessed that Mirror-Belle had run back to the gym with the squash ball – or was it really the magic ball? In either case, she had probably taken it back to her own land through one of the mirrors in the gym. But Ellen knew that to say so would be the wrong thing. It would only make Luke even crosser. So instead she asked, "Who won at squash?"

Luke scowled. That seemed to be the wrong thing too.

"I did," said Dad.

About the Author and Illustrator

Julia Donaldson is one of the UK's most popular children's writers. Her award-winning books include *What the Ladybird Heard, The Snail and the Whale* and *The Gruffalo*. She has also written many children's plays and songs, and her sell-out shows based on her books and songs are a huge success. She was the Children's Laureate from 2011 to 2013, campaigning for libraries and for deaf children, and creating a website for teachers called picturebookplays.co.uk. Julia and her husband Malcolm divide their time between Sussex and Edinburgh. You can find out more about Julia at www.juliadonaldson.co.uk.

Lydia Monks studied Illustration at Kingston University, graduating in 1994 with a first-class degree. She is a former winner of the Smarties Bronze Award for *I Wish I Were a Dog* and has illustrated many books by Julia Donaldson. Her illustrations have been widely admired.